KAY THOMPSON'S ELOISE
Eloise and the Dinosaurs

STORY BY **Lisa McClatchy**

ILLUSTRATED BY **Tammie Lyon**

Peachtree
Ready-to-Read

Simon Spotlight
New York   London   Toronto   Sydney   New Delhi

SIMON SPOTLIGHT

An imprint of Simon & Schuster Children's Publishing Division

1230 Avenue of the Americas, New York, NY 10020

First Simon Spotlight hardcover edition September 2017

First Aladdin Paperbacks edition January 2007

For information about special discounts for bulk purchases, please contact Simon & Schuster
Special Sales at 1-866-506-1949 or business@simonandschuster.com.

The text of this book was set in Century Old Style.

Manufactured in the United States of America 0817 LAK

2 4 6 8 10 9 7 5 3 1

Library of Congress Cataloging-in-Publication Data

McClatchy, Lisa.

Eloise and the dinosaurs / story by Lisa McClatchy ; illustrated by Tammie Lyon.—
1st Aladdin Paperbacks ed.

p. cm.—(Kay Thompson's Eloise) (Ready-to-read)

Summary: Phillip takes Eloise to the Museum of Natural History
to learn about dinosaurs.

ISBN 978-1-4814-9980-4 (hc)

ISBN 978-0-689-87453-6 (pbk)

[1. Dinosaurs—Fiction. 2. American Museum of Natural History—Fiction.
3. Museums—Fiction. 4. New York (N.Y.)—Fiction.] I. Lyon, Tammie, ill.
II. Thompson, Kay 1911- III. Title. IV. Series V. Series: Ready-to-read.

PZ7.M47841375Ekd 2006

[E]—dc22

I am Eloise.
I am a city child.

I have a tutor.
His name is Philip.
He is boring, boring, boring.

Today
Philip is taking me
to the museum.

We are going
to see the dinosaurs.

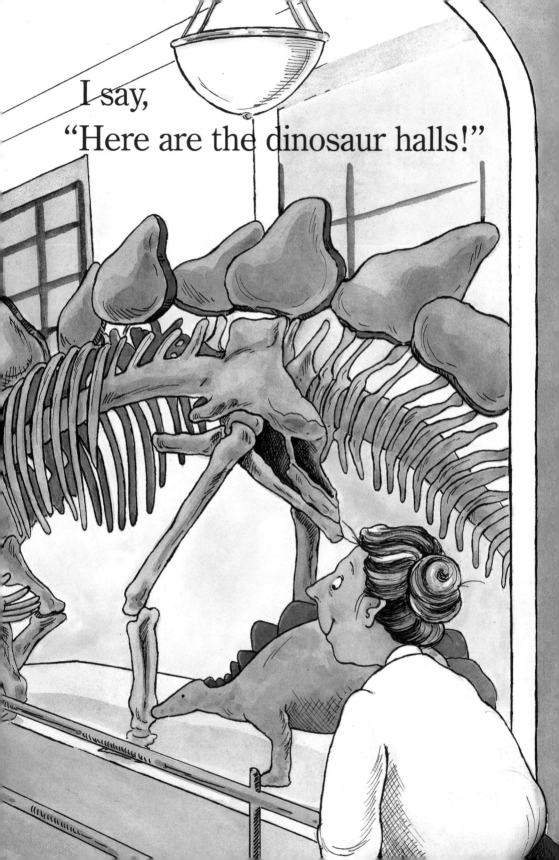

And he says,
"Please behave, Eloise."

And I say,
"Please behave, Eloise."

And he says,
"Here is a dinosaur."

And I say,
"Here is a dinosaur."

Philip says,
"It is a Tyrannosaurus rex."

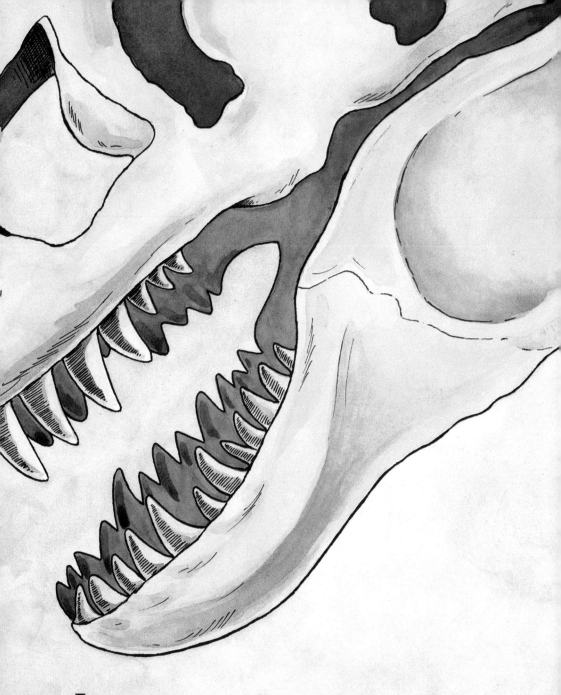

I say,
"It is a Tyrannosaurus rex."

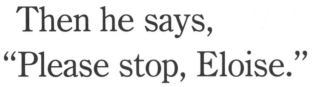

Then he says,
"Please stop, Eloise."

Then I say,
"Please stop, Eloise."

And he says,
"Nanny, make her stop!"

Nanny says,
"No, no, no, Eloise!"

I skip over to
the triceratops.

My pink bow
looks just right
on his horn.

I cartwheel over to
the apatosaurus.

He needs a hat.

Philip says,
"Eloise, do not touch
the dinosaurs!"

Then Nanny says,
"Eloise,
leave the dinosaurs alone.
It is time for lunch."

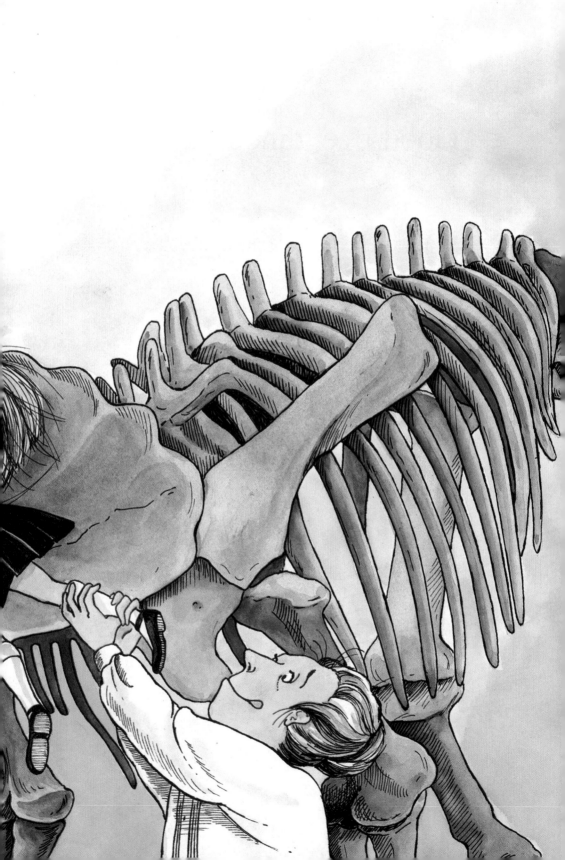

I say,
"Good-bye, dinosaurs."

Oh I love, love, love
dinosaurs!